VOTE!

by Diana G. Gallagher

illustrated by Brann Garvey

Librarian Reviewer
Laurie K. Holland
Media Specialist (National Board Certified), Edina, MN
MA in Elementary Education, Minnesota State University, Mankato

Reading Consultant
Sherry Klehr
Elementary/Middle School Educator, Edina Public Schools, MN
MA in Education, University of Minnesota

STONE ARCH BOOKS
www.stonearchbooks.com

Claudia Cristina Cortez is published by Stone Arch Books
151 Good Counsel Drive, P.O. Box 669
Mankato, Minnesota 56002
www.stonearchbooks.com

Library of Congress Cataloging-in-Publication Data
Gallagher, Diana G.
    Vote!: The Complicated Life of Claudia Cristina Cortez / by Diana G.
Gallagher; illustrated by Brann Garvey.
    p. cm. — (Claudia Cristina Cortez)
    ISBN 978-1-4342-0770-8 (library binding)
    ISBN 978-1-4342-0866-8 (pbk.)
    [1. Elections—Fiction. 2. Middle schools—Fiction. 3. Schools—Fiction.]
I. Garvey, Brann, ill. II. Title.
PZ7.G13543Vo 2009
[Fic]—dc22   2008004396

Summary: Claudia is the campaign manager for her friend Peter. Everyone else is
playing dirty to win class president. Can Peter win if he doesn't play dirty?

Art Director: Heather Kindseth
Graphic Designer: Kay Fraser

Photo Credits
Delaney Photography, cover, 1

        Printed in the United States of America in Stevens Point, Wisconsin.
082009
0005601R

Table of Contents

Cast of

ME

CLAUDIA

That's me. I'm thirteen, and I'm in the seventh grade at Pine Tree Middle School. I live with my mom, my dad, and my brother, Jimmy. I have one cat, Ping-Ping. I like music, baseball, and hanging out with my friends.

MONICA is my very best friend. We met when we were really little, and we've been best friends ever since. I don't know what I'd do without her! Monica loves horses. In fact, when she grows up, she wants to be an Olympic rider!

MONICA

BECCA

BECCA is one of my closest friends. She lives next door to Monica. Becca is really, really smart. She gets good grades. She's also really good at art.

ADAM and I met when we were in third grade. Now that we're teenagers, we don't spend as much time together as we did when we were kids, but he's always there for me when I need him. (Plus, he's the only person who wants to talk about baseball with me!)

ADAM

Characters

TOMMY's our class clown. Sometimes he's really funny, but sometimes he is just annoying. Becca has a crush on him . . . but I'd never tell.

I think **PETER** is probably the smartest person I've ever met. Seriously. He's even smarter than our teachers! He's also one of my friends. Which is lucky, because sometimes he helps me with homework.

Every school has a bully, and **JENNY** is ours. She's the tallest person in our class, and the meanest, too. She always threatens to stomp people. No one's ever seen her stomp anyone, but that doesn't mean it hasn't happened!

ANNA is the most popular girl at our school. Everyone wants to be friends with her. I think that's weird, because Anna can be really, really mean. I mostly try to stay away from her.

Cast of

CARLY is Anna's best friend. She always tries to act exactly like Anna does. She even wears the exact same clothes. She's never really been mean to me, but she's never been nice to me either!

NICK is my annoying seven-year-old neighbor. I get stuck babysitting him a lot. He likes to make me miserable. (Okay, he's not that bad ALL of the time . . . just most of the time.)

BRAD is a football star at my school. He's also really nice. And really cute. And really funny. If it sounds like I have a crush on him, it's because I do. But no one knows except Monica and Becca, and they'd never tell.

Characters

SYLVIA really wants to be Anna's friend. I don't know why, since Anna isn't ever nice to her.

SYLVIA

MS. STARK

MS. STARK is my history teacher at school. She's also my homeroom teacher. She's pretty nice, and she thinks I'm a good student.

JIMMY

JIMMY is my big brother. I stay out of his way, and he stays out of mine.

PRINCIPAL PAUL

PRINCIPAL PAUL is our school principal. Luckily, I've never had to go to his office!

CHAPTER 1

Peter Please

Some things at Pine Tree Middle School are different from Pine Tree Elementary School:

1. Switching rooms for classes.

2. Sitting wherever you want at lunch.

3. You don't have to walk in lines.

And some things are the same:

1. Math and English are required.

2. No T-shirts with words.

3. No running in the halls.

One thing is exactly the same: Elections.

Like my dad says, "**Some things never change.**"

When **Ms. Stark** announced that the seventh grade election season would start the next day, I wasn't the only one who groaned.

Adam did, too. Monica rolled her eyes. Becca just sighed.

Tommy is the class clown. He rolled his eyes, sighed, and GROANED.

Ms. Stark said, "You can nominate your choices tomorrow during lunch."

* * *

"Why do we bother having an election?" I asked Monica and Becca as we walked to first period.

"We have the election to choose a class president," **Monica** said.

"But the same kids always run," I reminded her. "And one of them always wins."

"And then the **winner doesn't do the job,**" **Becca** said.

"That's right," Monica said. "Why do they do that?"

"I don't know," Becca said. "But it's annoying. We spend a lot of time thinking about the election, and then afterward, they don't even care."

I sighed. "It's because everyone runs for *bad reasons*," I told them.

Bad Reasons People Run

Anna Dunlap *(our popular princess)*: She thinks she's better than everybody at everything. She won in fifth grade and acted like she had been elected queen.

Jenny Pinski *(our school bully)*: She runs because it makes everyone nervous. It was a huge surprise when she won last year. She quit after two weeks. Then Brad Turino took over.

Brad Turino *(our sports star)*: He thinks winning proves that everybody likes him. Everybody does like him. Brad is good-looking, a nice guy, and a sports star. He was president in fourth grade, and stepped in when Jenny quit last year.

"I think the seventh grade should vote for someone who will be the best class president," I told my friends. "Not just the most POPULAR or the COOLEST."

"Yeah, but who?" Monica asked.

I had an idea, but I didn't say anything. I didn't want to jinx it. It might just be CRAZY enough to work.

* * *

After school, I found my friend **Peter** in the library.

I sat down next to him, took a deep breath, and said, "I think you should run for class president, Peter."

Peter is shy, and sometimes he stutters. He was so SHOCKED he couldn't speak at all! He just stared at me.

"I'm serious," I went on. "We need someone who will do a good job. You."

Peter blinked.

"I'll be your campaign manager," I said.

Peter finally found his voice. "I can't, Claudia," he told me.

"Why not?" I asked. "You're the smartest kid in the whole school."

"I know." Peter sighed. "I get teased for being a brain. But the thing is, I get **tongue-tied** talking to strangers."

"You just have to shake hands and smile," I said.

Peter frowned, but it seemed like he was thinking about it.

"Being class president would look great on your **permanent record**," I added. Most middle school students worry about their next report card. Peter worries about getting into a great college.

"Good point," Peter said. "Just having straight As and being in the Science Club isn't enough."

"And you don't do **sports**," I added.

Peter nodded. Then he sighed and shook his head. "Sorry, Claudia. It would be too **humiliating** to lose."

"You might not lose," I said. "You won't know unless you try." I knew I was being pushy, but it was important.

Peter thought for a while. His forehead got all scrunched up, so I could tell he was thinking really hard.

"Okay," he finally said. "I'll run, but you have to promise something."

"What?" I said. I held my breath.

"If you **nominate** me, you can't ask anyone to second it," Peter said. "**Not even my friends.**"

I had forgotten about **seconding.** It wasn't enough to just nominate someone. When you chose a candidate, someone else had to say that they chose them too. That was called **seconding.**

It was weird that Peter didn't want his friends to second his nomination.

"Why not?" I asked.

"I want someone to second because I'll be the best president," Peter explained.

I wasn't worried about it. Every person who is nominated gets a second. ALWAYS. There was nothing to worry about.

I raised my right hand.

"I promise," I said.

Peter and I shook on it. And everyone knows that **when Claudia Cristina Cortez makes a promise, she never goes back on her word.**

CHAPTER 2

Seconds Anyone?

The next day, Peter and I sat with our friends at lunch.

Nobody knew I was going to nominate Peter for class president.

"I got kicked at football practice yesterday," Adam said. "Three times!"

"No wonder the Cougars always lose," Tommy said. "They mix up the BALL and the boys."

"The Cougars don't always lose," Monica said, frowning.

Monica and I have been best friends since kindergarten. She goes along with all my crazy ideas, and she doesn't get mad if we get into trouble.

"Tommy didn't really mean **always,**" Becca said.

"Right," **Tommy** agreed. "I meant almost always."

Becca giggled.

Becca is my other best friend. She has a crush on Tommy, but only Monica and I know about it.

"There's **Principal Paul,**" Monica said, pointing to the front of the cafeteria.

I had **butterflies in my stomach.** It was time to nominate people for class president.

Peter pushed his glasses back on his nose. Then he sat up very straight and very still.

A football player nominated **Brad Turino.** The whole team raised their hands to second it. That meant Brad was running for president.

Boys always vote for Brad because he's a good athlete. They think he's a *hero or something.*

"Brad is too busy with sports. He only went to three meetings last year," Monica said. "What kind of president is that?"

"A missing one," Tommy joked. "Brad didn't call in sick. He called in sports."

We all grinned.

Then Carly Madison nominated Anna Dunlap.

We all groaned.

Anna is the most popular girl in school. I don't know why. No one really likes her.

Anna is bossy, and she makes other people do all the work. Most of the girls vote for her anyway.

The girl who nominated **Jenny Pinski** looked kind of scared. But then, everyone's afraid of Jenny. That's why a lot of kids vote for her.

Jenny is always threatening to stomp kids who make her mad. And it would make her mad to know that someone hadn't voted for her.

I've never voted for Jenny. I guess she never found out, since I've never been STOMPED.

(Actually, Jenny's never stomped anyone that I know of, but who wants to take the chance?)

"Anyone else?" Principal Paul asked.

Peter swallowed hard.

I called out, "I nominate **Peter Wiggins.**"

The whole cafeteria got quiet.

"An **excellent** choice, Claudia," **Principal**
Paul said. He smiled.

I almost fell off my chair! Principal Paul never smiles. He never frowns, either. Usually, I can't tell when he's MAD or GLAD.

"Who wants to second Peter?" the principal asked.

Tommy started to raise his hand. "No," I told him. I looked at the kids at our table. "None of us can. Peter wants someone else to do it."

My friends looked **puzzled**, but they didn't raise their hands.

Peter pushed his glasses again. He does that when he's nervous.

My stomach flip-flopped. It does that when I'm nervous. If someone didn't raise their hand soon, Peter couldn't run for president.

The seconds ticked by.

Tick . . . tick . . . tick . . . TICK!

Everyone glanced around the room.

"Well," Principal Paul said. "If no one seconds—"

"Me!" Kyle Larson jumped out of his seat. **Kyle** is the shortest kid in the whole school. He's hard to see, even when he's standing up. "I second!" he yelled.

"Yes!" I shouted. It was **official.** Peter was a candidate for president of the seventh grade.

"Good luck in your campaigns," Principal Paul said. "Remember, each candidate will need to prepare a speech for the assembly, which is going to take place this Thursday. Everyone is expected to vote in the election, which will take place a week from Friday."

Peter looked worried. "Don't worry," I told him. "With Claudia Cortez managing your **campaign,** you're going to be great!"

CAMPAIGN MANAGER
Claudia

But suddenly, I wasn't so sure.

CHAPTER 3

Campaign Committee

All of Peter's friends wanted to work on his campaign. Peter was THRILLED. "I need lots of help!" he told us.

"Let's meet at my **tree house** after school," I said.

My dad built the tree house for my older brother when Jimmy was really little. Since he's sixteen now, Jimmy doesn't use it, so I do. It would be a great campaign headquarters.

"What should we do first?" Peter asked.

"We have to make '**Vote For Peter**' signs," I said. "They will advertise your campaign."

* * *

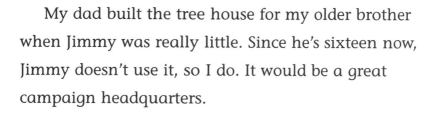

Becca and I walked home together after school. We stopped at her house to pick up **poster board and markers.** Becca wants to be an ARTIST, so she always has art supplies.

Becca had plans for the posters.

Peter's signs had to:

* Be great

* Be colorful

* Be funny

* Have his face all over them

* Make him win!

Peter was waiting in my backyard when we arrived. But he was alone. Adam, Tommy, and Monica weren't there.

"I'm sure they have **good reasons**," I said.

"Probably," Peter said. He didn't sound like he believed it.

"Claudia!" my mom called from the back door.

I gave Peter the art supplies. He and Becca went to the tree house.

I had a **bad feeling** when I walked into the kitchen. And my bad feeling was right. Mom wanted me to watch Nick.

Nick Wright is seven years old.

He is DISGUSTING. He is *annoying*. He is a **total brat.** And he is my **next-door neighbor.**

Nick's mom is really busy, so he stays at our house a lot. I have to watch him almost every day. My mom pays me **$2.00** an hour, but it isn't enough. A **million dollars** an hour wouldn't be enough to watch Nick.

"We're having a campaign committee meeting, Nick," I said, leading him to the back yard. "So try to be good, okay?"

"What's a campaign?" Nick asked.

"All the stuff we have to do to get Peter elected president of the seventh grade," I explained. "All his **friends** are on the committee."

"What's a committee?" Nick asked.

"The people helping Peter," I explained.

"What's a people?" Nick asked.

I rolled my eyes. "Now you're just being **annoying,**" I told him.

Nick and I climbed into the tree house.

"What's going on?" Peter asked.

"I have to watch Nick while my mom's busy," I said.

Becca gasped. "Right now?" she said. "But we're doing something important."

My best friends know all about Nick. He's famous for being the neighborhood pest.

Nick looked at Becca, then at me. "Is this all of Peter's friends? The whole committee? Just you two?" he asked.

"No. There are five people on Peter's committee," I said.

"Three couldn't come," Becca added.

"That's a bad sign, isn't it?" **Peter** said. He looked worried. "Maybe I should QUIT now, before the campaign gets started."

Nick laughed and said, in a singsong voice, "Peter is a quitter. Peter is a quitter."

"Stop it, Nick," I yelled. "That's not nice."

"Don't be mad at Nick," Peter said. "He's right."

Nick blinked. "I am?" he asked quietly.

Peter nodded. "If I back out now, the kids at school will think I'm a quitter, too," he explained.

"You're right. **Dropping out** could be worse than **losing,**" I said.

"Are you running or quitting, Peter?" Nick asked.

"Running," Peter said. "Hey, Nick, do you want to help with my campaign?"

Becca and I both shook our heads like crazy. Nick is loud, and he won't sit still. He **lies** to get out of trouble, and he **wrecks things.** I guess Peter didn't know that. Or maybe he didn't care.

Nick's eyes lit up. "Can I? Really?" he asked.

"Sure," Peter said. "We're making signs."

"Cool!" Nick yelled. He sat down next to Becca. She handed him a box of markers. Then he waited — quietly!

I was shocked.

"We need SLOGANS for the signs," Becca said.

"They have to be **honest,**" Peter said.

"Totally honest?" I asked. I knew that the other kids would probably **lie** to get votes. But this was Peter's campaign. He had the final say.

"Totally," Peter said. He straightened the art supplies. Then he took his markers out of the box and started to put them back.

"What are you doing?" Nick asked.

"I'm putting the colors in **rainbow order,**" Peter explained. "Red, orange, yellow, green, blue, and purple."

Nick put all his markers in rainbow order too.

"Do you like this?" Becca asked. She held up a paper that said:

He's a brain! He wears glasses!

He's clumsy and shy.

Vote Peter for President.

He's the nicest guy!

"I knew you were a great artist, Becca," Peter said. "I didn't know you were a great poet, too!"

"I love it!" I exclaimed.

"Here's another one," **Becca** said. She  held up a second piece of paper.

He's not the coolest,

But he's the smartest.

Vote Peter for President,

He's kind and honest!

"Perfect," Peter said.

Then we got busy making signs.

Everyone had a different style. My letters were big and bold. Becca put sweeping tails on her capitals. All of Peter's letters were exactly the same size. Some of Nick's letters were **backward,** but we didn't say anything. It was cool that all of the posters looked **different** from each other.

We had a great time. I loved the campaign slogans that Becca had written. Everyone made cool, colorful posters. We didn't even get mad when Nick made up tunes for Peter's slogans and sang them over and over all afternoon.

In fact, the rest of us even started to SING ALONG!

Stolen Slogans

Becca, Peter, and I went to school early on Wednesday morning. We wanted to hang up Peter's signs before **the first bell rang.**

Monica, Adam, and Tommy showed up too.

"Where were you guys yesterday?" I asked.

"I had to go to football practice," Adam said. "If I miss practice, Coach won't let me play in the game Saturday. He might even kick me off the team. I'm sorry, Peter."

"I had a **dentist appointment,**" Monica explained. "Believe me, Peter. I'd rather make signs."

"Me, too," Tommy agreed. "My mom made me *mow the lawn.*"

"That's okay," Peter said. "You're all here now."

"Let's go before all the best spots are taken," I said. A good campaign manager keeps things *MOVING.*

First, we headed to the **bulletin board**  right outside the cafeteria. Everyone sees it every day.

But **Sylvia** had gotten there first. That was bad news. Sylvia is FAMOUS for being **really, really slow.**

She was slowly hanging up a poster for Anna. "Will you be long, Sylvia?" I asked. There was room on the bulletin board for one more poster.

"Just a few more seconds," Sylvia said. She held Anna's poster in place.

She carefully pushed in a tack. Then she picked up another tack. She did it all in *slow motion.*

She wasn't trying to be rude. She's just sort of slow. That's just how Sylvia is.

"Take your time," Tommy said.

Monica poked him in the ribs.

"I will," Sylvia said. "**Anna** wants everything to be just right."

Sylvia tries really hard to get Anna to like her. It doesn't work. *Anna ignores her* most of the time.

"Okay, I'm done," Sylvia said finally.

She moved away so that we could see the **poster.**

Peter, Becca, and I gasped.

Anna's poster read:

She's pretty and witty,

a popular snob!

Vote Anna for President.

She's the best one for the job!

The words were different, but the idea was the same. It was honest about Anna. Just like Peter's posters were **honest** about him!

"What does that one say?" Adam asked, sounding worried. He pointed down the hall.

Carly, Anna's best friend, was standing by the principal's office. She finished hanging up another poster and walked away. We all ran to look.

She's cute and cool,
and kind of smart.
Vote Anna for President.
She's honest, with heart.

"Anna's slogans are just like Peter's!" **Becca**  exclaimed.

"How did that happen?" Monica asked.

"I don't know," I said. "But something  is FISHY."

"Now we can't hang my posters," Peter said.

"Why not?" Adam asked.

"Because **everyone** will think I copied Anna," Peter explained.

Peter was right. Nobody would accuse the most popular girl in school of COPYING.

"Now what do we do?" Tommy threw up his hands.

"Make more signs," Peter said.

Adam winced. "I have practice again today," he said.

"My mom is getting **her hair done**," **Monica** said. "I have to watch my little sister."

"And I have to *mow my backyard*,"
Tommy told us. He sighed. "I only
got about **half of it** done yesterday."

"That's okay," Becca said. "We need new slogans
anyway, before we can make more posters."

I needed to figure out how *Anna* had found out
about *Peter's* campaign slogans.

CHAPTER 5

Leak

I walked home with Becca after school. The *stolen slogan mystery* was on my mind.

"How did Anna find out what Peter's signs said?" I wondered out loud. "Nobody could possibly hear us. We were in the **tree house!**"

"I know," Becca agreed. "That's why it's a great meeting place."

There was only **one explanation** for what had happened.

Someone on our committee must have told Anna or someone on her committee.

"Did you *tell anyone* about your ideas?" I asked.

"No!" Becca said. She stopped walking and turned so that she was looking at me. "I didn't 𝓑𝓡𝓐𝓖 or 𝓑𝓛𝓐𝓑 to Anna or her friends or to anyone. How could you think that?"

"I didn't mean you did it on purpose," I explained.

Becca was too UPSET to listen. "I don't want to work on Peter's campaign anymore," she said. Then she started walking away really fast.

"Becca, wait!" I called, but she kept walking. I wanted to go after her, but I couldn't. I had to find out how Anna had stolen Peter's slogans.

I was *depressed* when I got home.

"What's wrong, honey?" **my mom** asked when I walked into the living room.

I sighed. "Well, some of our campaign secrets got out," I told her. "And I can't figure it out. Someone must have told someone on the other campaigns."

"You mean there's a leak?" my mom asked.

I pictured the **leaky faucet** in our bathroom. If the campaign secrets were the water, and the committee was the pipes, then the leaky faucet was whoever told the secret.

"That sounds right," I told my mom.

"Well, that should be easy enough," my mom said. "You just need to find the leak, and fix it!"

I sighed again.

The leaky faucet in our bathroom had been leaking for years.

Obviously, it was *harder to fix a leak* than my mom thought.

I went into the kitchen and called Peter.

"We have to figure out where the leak is," I told him. "Are you sure you didn't tell anyone about the slogans?"

"I didn't talk to **anyone** after the meeting," Peter told me. "Not even Adam and Tommy."

"I didn't really think so," I explained. "But we have to find the leak before our next meeting, or Anna might find out all our secrets."

"Well, Monica wasn't at the meeting," Peter said. "That leaves **Nick.**"

Nick doesn't know anyone at middle school besides me and my friends. But I had to check him out.

I went over to Nick's house. **Mrs. Wright** answered the door.

"Hi, Mrs. Wright. Did Nick talk to anyone after he came home yesterday?" I asked. "Besides you and his dad?"

"No," *Nick's mom* said. "He didn't even do much talking with us. He just sang those silly songs, over and over and over!"

The slogans.

But Nick's mom and dad couldn't be the leaks. They didn't know any middle-school students.

If Nick wasn't the leak, who was? I wondered as I walked home.

It hit me when I walked in the front door.

Nick likes to watch my brother play video games. After our campaign committee meeting, he had gone into Jimmy's room for a while to watch him play. And Jimmy knows Anna's older brother, Ben.

I put the pieces together in my head.

1. Nick sang the songs to Jimmy.

2. Jimmy must have figured out that the songs were campaign slogans.

3. Jimmy was mad at me because I told my parents that he had a girlfriend (even though he didn't).

4. To get back at me, Jimmy told Ben the slogans.

5. Then Ben told Anna!

I barged into Jimmy's room. He was at his **computer**.

"Did you hear Nick singing Peter's campaign slogans yesterday?" I asked.

"No." Jimmy turned to look at me. "I heard you singing Peter's campaign slogans."

I thought he was KIDDING. Then I remembered.

Nick sang Peter's slogans over and over at the meeting. **I couldn't get the songs out of my head.** I was singing them all evening. And Jimmy's door was wide open.

"Did you tell Anna's brother what I sang?" I asked. I was shocked. How could my own brother **betray** me?

"No," Jimmy said. "**You did.**"

I gasped. "I did?" I whispered.

Jimmy nodded.

"I didn't talk to Ben," I said.

"You kind of did," Jimmy said. "My speakerphone was on."

Jimmy and Ben talk while they play games together online. They use speakerphones so their hands are free to play.

Anna's brother heard me singing on his speakerphone.

In fact, if Ben could hear me, Anna could have heard me.

I was the leak!

CHAPTER 6

Blame Game

At school the next morning, I found *Peter* in the library. I ran over to him and whispered, "*I'm the leak!* I couldn't stop singing Nick's songs."

Then I told him the whole story.

Peter understood. "I couldn't get the songs out of my head, either," he told me.

"But you didn't sing them into a speakerphone," I said.

"No," Peter agreed. "But you didn't know that it was on."

I sighed. Even if it was a mistake, **I felt terrible.**

"It's not your fault," Peter added.

"Yes, it is," I said. "Plus, I *hurt Becca's feelings* yesterday when I asked her if she told anyone the slogans. Now she wants to quit the committee. I feel 𝔸𝕎𝔽𝕌𝕃. I didn't mean to make her mad."

"But Becca makes the best signs," Peter said.

"I know," I said. I took a deep breath. I knew what I had to do. Quietly, I said, **"I'm a terrible campaign manager. You should kick me off the committee."**

Peter laughed. Then he said, *"No way.* We're in this together."

I was really **relieved** Peter didn't blame me. But that didn't solve our problem.

"I'm going to BEG Becca to come back," I said.

"I'll help," Peter told me. "This is my campaign. If something goes wrong, it's my fault, too."

We put a note in Becca's locker.

Dear Becca,

Please don't quit the campaign committee. We need you! You make the best posters. Claudia didn't mean to hurt your feelings. She feels awful! Don't leave, Becca!

Sincerely,

Claudia and Peter

At lunch, Becca ran over to me. "I knew you didn't think I hurt Peter's campaign on purpose," Becca said. "I was just UPSET."

"So you're not going to QUIT?" I asked.

"No way!" Becca said, laughing. "I have more great slogans."

"Shhh!" I put my finger to my lips. Then I whispered, "Don't say a word until we get to the tree house after school!"

* * *

Everyone came to the meeting except Adam. He had football practice again. Unfortunately, **Nick** was at my house when we got there.

"Can I make more signs?" Nick asked.

"Only if you promise not to sing," Peter said, smiling.

Nick looked **crushed.** "You don't like my singing?" he asked quietly.

"No," Peter said. He smiled at Nick and added, "But I **love** your signs!"

Nick stuck out his lower lip, but he didn't stamp his foot. That meant he was only *sort of mad.*

"Is your speech ready, Peter?" Monica asked.

"Oh, no!" Peter exclaimed. "**I forgot all about that!**"

There was a special assembly the next day at school. All the candidates had to give a speech.

"Don't **panic,**" I said. "We have a whole day."

"I'll help you write it," Monica offered.

"You'll need a joke. How's this?" Tommy cleared his throat. "I'm running for president. **Bet you can't catch me!**"

Nick laughed. No one else did. Everyone looked worried about Peter's speech.

"No jokes," Peter said. "I'm not the FUNNY type."

"What do you want the speech to say?" Monica asked.

Peter shrugged. "I just need to make sure it's honest. And short," he told her.

"Use all the reasons Peter should be president," I said.

"He's smart, but **he doesn't brag**," Becca said.

"And he's nice to everyone," Monica added. "Even if he's too shy to talk a lot."

"**Peter is neater**," Nick blurted out.

Peter blinked. Then he smiled. "That's pretty good, Nick!" he said.

Nick's slogan was true. Peter was very neat. He organized all his stuff. His **locker** wasn't messy, and his clothes *never* had stains on them.

"Let's use that on the new posters," Becca suggested.

Nick gave Peter a HIGH FIVE.

I felt a lot better. The day started with a campaign crisis. It ended with a **fabulous** slogan. And no one was mad. Not even Nick.

Maybe I wasn't a bad campaign manager after all!

CHAPTER 7

Pander and Promise

The next day at lunch, I stopped outside the cafeteria. A bunch of kids were looking at one of Peter's new posters.

Peter's Presidential Report Card

[X]   Smart

      Cool

[X]   Perfect attendance

      Detention

Who would make a better president:
A smart kid who shows up . . .
Or a cool kid who goofs off?

My friends were already sitting at our table.

"Anna is freaking out," Becca whispered. She grinned. "She absolutely hates the 'cool kid' poster."

"She's not happy about the 'Peter is neater' sign, either," Adam said.

Jenny is tough. Anna is sweeter.

Peter for President. Peter is neater!

"Too bad for Anna," I said. "She shouldn't have stolen our first ideas."

Peter didn't say anything. He was reading a piece of paper.

"Well?" Monica asked.

"I can't use this in my speech," Peter said.

"Why not?" Monica asked. "I thought it was really good!"

"It makes PROMISES I can't keep," Peter explained. "And it **panders** to special groups."

"I don't even know what pander means," Monica said.

Peter tried to explain.

"It means that it tries to make people vote for me by telling them that I'll *do something* that will help them," he told us. "Like, the speech promises the science kids that I'll use the money we collect from recycling cans to get new stuff for the science lab. That's *pandering* to the science club."

Monica looked puzzled. "You told me the science club wants new microscopes," she said.

"I'm running to be president of the whole seventh grade," Peter said. "I can't promise something for everyone."

"The other candidates will," I said.

"But **they won't keep the promises**," Peter argued.

"That won't matter after the election," Tommy said.

"It would matter to me," Peter said. "If I win, I want to win by being honest."

Peter's Promises

1. Give the soda can money to charity

2. Get kids to pick up litter

"Asking kids to work won't win votes," Adam said.

"You have to promise something fun," Tommy said.

Peter paused. Then he snapped his fingers. "T-shirt Tuesday once a month!" he exclaimed. "When we can wear shirts that have words on them."

"I like it," I said, "but it's against the dress code."

"Principal Paul might try it," Becca said. "As long as the shirts don't have bad stuff on them, once a month might be okay."

"It'll sound GOOD in the speech," Monica pointed out.

"That's another thing I'm worried about," Peter admitted. "The speech won't sound good if I stutter."

"You won't," I said. But I wasn't sure. Peter stuttered a lot — even when he talked in class. And he would be giving his speech to all the kids in seventh grade!

Peter would be the best class president ever. If I could get him elected.

CHAPTER 8

The Big Speech

Peter was **really nervous** before his speech. I wouldn't let him look at the crowd. That would just make it worse.

"I'll be in the front row," I told him, "with all your friends. Just pretend **we're the only people there.**"

"Okay," Peter croaked. His voice sounded HOARSE. "I need more water," he told me, pointing at his throat.

"You've gone to the drinking fountain five times in ten minutes," I said.

"**My throat is dry,**" Peter explained.

"Hurry," I said. "The speeches are about to start."

I waited until Peter got back.

I gave him a hug and told him to *relax.*

Then I sat down next to Adam and took **notes.**

Speech Notes

Anna: Pretty dress, perfect hair. Sounds confident (and phony).

Promises:

1. Use can $ to send cheerleaders to state competition.

2. Play music during study hall.

3. Use main bulletin board for "Teen Fads & Trends."

Everyone applauded when Anna finished. Anna has a lot of power.

Jenny: Talks tough, shakes her fist, gives everyone the "Jenny Pinski stare."

Promises:

1. Use soda can $ for a class pizza party.

2. School store should give paper and pencils for free.

3. Everyone should get three warnings before getting detention.

The crowd cheered and whistled for Jenny.

We all knew she wouldn't be able to do any of the things she promised. We clapped because she was watching.

Brad: Looks really cute!

Promise:

1. Use can $ for new football helmets with school logo.

Brad's speech was short, but everyone loved it, because everyone loves Brad.

My stomach started to hurt when Peter walked out. I crossed my fingers and smiled, but Peter didn't see me. He stared at his speech.

I took more notes.

Peter: Talks too quietly. Microphone screeches. Starts to sweat. Jiggles constantly. Stutters.

Suddenly, Peter started talking really fast. He raced through the speech like he was afraid to stop or breathe!

Promises:

1. Give soda can $ to charity.

2. Pick up litter on school grounds.

I waited for Peter to mention T-shirt Tuesday, but he didn't. He just ran off the stage.

I heard giggles and whispers. Only a few people clapped.

Everyone thought Peter ran away because he was scared.

I was pretty sure he just had to use the **bathroom.** He drank a lot of water before his speech!

CHAPTER 9

Working Weekend

We had another campaign meeting on Saturday. I was the last one there because I had Nick with me.

Becca groaned.

"Nick's mom and dad are playing **tennis**," I explained.

"I'm glad to see you, Nick," Peter said, smiling. He wasn't lying. He really liked Nick. Nick liked Peter too.

"Where are Adam and Monica?" I asked.

"Adam has a football game," Tommy said.

"Monica went to a **wedding**," Becca explained.

"What's this meeting for anyway?" Tommy asked. "Peter already has **a million posters** up at school."

"This is a planning meeting," I said. "There are two more events before we vote on Friday."

"Right. Meet the Candidates, and the debate," **Becca** said.

"What's a **debate?**" Nick asked.

"It's like *an argument with rules,*" Peter explained. "You can't yell at the other guy."

"Oh," Nick said. "I get it. Is it hard?"

"Debates are easy," Peter said. "Meeting people is the hard part."

"Why is meeting people hard?" Nick asked.

"I get nervous when I talk to kids I don't know," Peter admitted.

"Oh," Nick said. He thought hard for a minute. "Why don't you give away **cookies?** People can't talk when they're CHEWING."

"I don't want to **buy votes,**" Peter said.

"The other candidates are giving away stuff," I said.

"Giving cookies is **bribery,**" Peter said. "Let's just hand out **stickers that say 'Vote For Peter.'** That's enough."

I didn't argue. **Peter's mind was made up.** And we had more to talk about.

I looked at my list. "There is going to be an **interview** for the school paper," I reminded him. "The reporter is going to call you tonight. Is that okay?"

Peter nodded. "I talk better on the phone," he said.

I sure hoped so. Peter needed a great interview in the *Pinecone Press*. Then maybe everyone would forget about his speedy speech getaway.

CHAPTER 10

Meet the Candidates

Every seventh grader came to the **Meet the Candidates party** on Monday.

Peter's table was in the corner. Monica hung red, white, and blue streamers on the front. Becca made piles of pieces of paper. The papers listed Peter's campaign promises. Becca and I had printed "Vote For Peter" on stickers. They were in a basket.

"**This looks great!**" Peter exclaimed. "I feel like a real candidate."

"You are a real candidate," I said.

"Real candidates don't get *tongue-tied* talking to anybody who isn't their friend," Peter said.

"I'll be right here with you to help," I promised. As long as Brad Turino didn't come over, I'd be fine. **I'd definitely get tongue-tied talking to Brad.**

Adam walked over. "I can't stay long," he told us. "I have practice. But I wanted to wish you luck, Peter."

"We'll need it," Tommy said. He looked gloomy. "Fliers and jokes can't compete with Anna's brownies."

"Jenny is giving away sour GUMBALLS," Adam said. He pulled a wrapped gumball out of his pocket. "I love these things."

"Brad is handing out signed pictures of himself," Monica said.

I gasped. "For real?"

Monica nodded. "All the girls are lining up."

I had to go to Brad's table before he ran out of photos, but I couldn't leave. I was Peter's campaign manager. He needed me for support, and so that he could talk to people without stuttering.

Thirty minutes passed, but only three kids came to Peter's table.

"Will you punch me if I don't vote for you?" Sofie Dominguez asked.

"No," Peter answered.

Sofie looked relieved. "Then I'd better vote for Jenny. Just to be safe," she said.

Then she walked away.

A few minutes later, Kyle tugged on Peter's shirt. He was so short that Peter had to look down.

"Hi, Kyle," Peter said, grinning. I guess Kyle didn't make him nervous. "Thanks for the second when Claudia nominated me," Peter went on. "Are you going to **vote for me?**"

"Will you put **a stool** by the water fountain in the gym?" Kyle asked. "Short kids can't reach it."

"I'll help you get a stool even if I don't win," Peter said.

Kyle smiled a huge smile. That made me smile too. Peter just had to get elected. *He was absolutely the best kid for the job.*

"I'm supposed to be spying for Jenny," Kristen said when she came over. She twirled the end of her ponytail. "But I think you'd make a better president, Peter."

Peter BLUSHED. "Uh, well, uh — thanks," he mumbled.

No one else stopped by.

"I'm going to hand out fliers," Becca said. Tommy went with her. Adam had already left for practice.

"You and Peter should walk around, Claudia," Monica said. "I'll watch the table."

We talked to several groups of kids. The conversation went like this every time:

1. I introduced Peter.

2. Peter mumbled something.

3. I told the kids about T-Shirt Tuesday.

4. Peter turned red.

5. I offered "Vote For Peter" stickers.

6. Most kids already had Anna's campaign buttons. They didn't want stickers.

7. Peter mumbled something else.

8. We moved on to the next group.

"I don't think this is working," Peter said.

"You have to LOOSEN UP, Peter!" I told him quietly. "Smile. Have fun. These kids don't bite."

Then I heard **Brad Turino's** voice.
He was talking to me! "Would you like a
picture, Claudia?" Brad asked.

My knees felt like jelly. I wobbled. I tried to
say yes. A squeaky noise came out instead.

"I saved one for you," Brad said. He held out a
photo. **His smile was dazzling.**

I froze. And then I got the HICCUPS!

Peter gave me a funny look. Then he took the
photo from Brad and gave it to me. "Here, Claudia."

HIC. HIC. I tried to smile, but I just kept
hiccupping.

I had to say something!
HIC. HIC.

If I timed it just right, I could say "thanks" between
hiccups. Just as I opened my mouth, another girl
walked up.

"Would you like a picture?" Brad asked the girl.

HIC!

I hiccupped really loud.

My face turned red and I ran.

I felt like crying. Peter ran after me and stopped me. He smiled kindly and said, "Don't be upset, Claudia. It's not a total disaster."

No, it was worse. I had acted like a total idiot in front of Brad Turino! It was a *catastrophe*. That's the **worst kind of disaster** there is!

"I don't feel as nervous anymore," Peter said.

"That's great!" I managed to say between hiccups. I looked around the room. It was too late. The students were leaving the cafeteria. Meet the Candidates was over.

CHAPTER 11

Muddy Politics

The *Pinecone Press* came out on Tuesday morning. I wanted to read Peter's interview right away. I found a stack of newspapers in the library. The interviews with all of the candidates were on the first page.

Anna's interview was first.

Reporter: Why would you make the best class president?

Anna: If the president looks good, the whole seventh grade looks good. I look fabulous all the time! Unlike the other girl running for president.

Reporter: What about doing the job?

Anna: A president has to make decisions. Brad is a great team player, but he follows his coach's orders. He doesn't give orders. That's one thing I'm great at!

Reporter: Do you have anything else to say?

Anna: I'm not afraid to speak up. Peter hardly ever talks to anyone.

My eyes popped out in SHOCK. Not way out like cartoon eyes, but close.

Anna's comment was mean, but it wasn't a lie. Peter does have trouble talking to people.

I read Jenny's interview next.

Reporter: Why should the seventh grade elect you?

Jenny: A president has to be tough. I'm tough.

Reporter: What else makes a good president?

Jenny: I'll tell you what makes a bad president. Anna is too stuck up. Brad is too busy. And Peter is a pushover.

Jenny made Peter sound like a WIMP!

That was so unfair. And it wasn't even true. Peter just didn't like to fight about stuff that wasn't important.

"What's wrong?" Monica asked, sitting down next to me.

"Read this," I said, giving her another copy of the newspaper.

Then I read Brad's interview.

Reporter: Why should you be president?

Brad: A president can't get anything done if nobody likes him. Everybody likes me.

Reporter: Don't kids like the other candidates?

Brad: Anna will forget about the people on her committee after the election. Everyone's afraid of Jenny. Peter is so smart that he makes everyone else feel stupid, even if he doesn't mean to.

Reporter: What about football? The Cougars need you to win.

Brad: If I'm elected, I promise I won't miss any practices.

I couldn't believe it. Brad had insulted Peter.

Did that mean I had to stop liking **Brad**? Would I be a bad friend if I couldn't stop liking him?

I didn't want to think about that, so I read Peter's interview.

Reporter: Why would you make a good president?

Peter: I'm smart. I show up, and I work hard.

Reporter: Do you think the other candidates are stupid and lazy?

Peter: No, not at all. I just know that I have qualities and skills that would make me a good class president.

Reporter: Do you have anything else to say?

Peter: No.

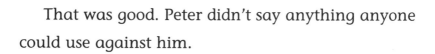

That was good. Peter didn't say anything anyone could use against him.

Peter rushed in and grabbed a copy of the newspaper. "How is it?" he asked. "Is it awful? Did I mess up?"

"No," Monica answered. "You didn't talk bad about anyone."

"But they all said **bad things** about you," I said loudly. "And everyone else."

The librarian gave me a look, but I didn't care. I was MAD. "You have to prove they're wrong at the debate," I told Peter.

"In front of everyone?" Peter asked. He looked terrified.

"It's the only way for you to win," I said.

VOTE
☐ WIN
☐ LOSE

CHAPTER 12

The Debate

The debate was held Wednesday afternoon. We all gathered in the school auditorium.

"Dan will ask the questions," **Principal Paul** said.

Dan Carter was the student editor of the *Pinecone Press.* He sat at the front of the stage. The candidates sat in the middle, facing Dan and the audience.

"I hope Peter doesn't **run off the stage** this time," Adam said.

"He won't," I said.

A campaign manager has to be 𝒯𝒪𝒰𝒢ℋ sometimes. I told Peter he couldn't drink anything all day. That solved the bathroom problem. But I couldn't do anything about Peter's nerves.

Peter crossed and uncrossed his feet, back and forth. He tapped his fingers on his knees. His face looked **sweaty.**

Dan blew into his microphone. Then he began.

Question: The president gets to decide what to put on the main bulletin board by the cafeteria. What would each of you use it for?

Anna: I would make a display of Teen Fads & Trends.

Jenny: I don't care about the bulletin board.

Brad: We can't give up sports displays.

Peter: I agree with Brad.

Peter's voice CRACKED. I heard some girls giggle. He coughed. Then I realized what was wrong.

His throat was too dry, because I wouldn't let him drink anything!

I had solved one problem and created another problem.

Principal Paul gave Peter a glass of water. He took a sip and tried again.

Peter: As I was saying, I agree with Brad. Every club and sports team should have a chance to use the main bulletin board. That's only fair.

Question: One of the candidates thinks the school store should give away pencils and paper for free to students. What do you think?

Jenny: I think it's a great idea!

Anna: The school store should sell combs and breath mints. And makeup.

Brad: We should also sell caps with the school logo.

Peter: The giveaway idea is nice, but it won't work. Paper and pencils cost money. Somebody has to pay for them.

The crowd gasped. Peter had just blasted Jenny's idea. In public!

I started to get worried.

What if Jenny **stomped** Peter before the election?

Dan went on to the next topic.

Question: As president, how will you get other kids to work with you?

Jenny: They'll do what I say or else!

Anna: Nobody turns down the most popular girl in school. Besides, all my friends want to work on projects that get them out of class.

Brad: Fans will do anything for a sports star.

Peter: I'm not tough, popular, or a star. But I'll work hard. Then everyone else will work hard, too. I won't give my friends projects just because they're fun. I'll pick the best kids for the job.

I sank even lower in my seat. Peter wasn't trying to lose. He was being honest. *But honesty doesn't win votes.* Peter might even come in last, behind Jenny Pinski!

But I **never give up.** Peter hadn't lost the election yet.

After school, I called an emergency meeting of the campaign committee.

CHAPTER 13

Advice and Action

As I walked home, **Mr. Gomez** called out, "Good afternoon, Claudia!"

Mr. Gomez lives across the street from me. He and his wife are kind of like grandparents to me. So I knew *I could talk to him* about what was going on.

"What's the matter?" Mr. Gomez asked. "You look sad."

I told him about Peter's problems.

After I was done with the entire story, I said, "He'll make the best class president, but everyone's going to vote for Brad, Jenny, or Anna. **For stupid reasons.**"

"Voters don't always tell people what they really think," Mr. Gomez said. "Peter might have lots of votes *you don't know about.*"

I didn't want to get my hopes up. But Mr. Gomez could be right. Nobody would tell Jenny or Anna they were voting for someone else.

"Thanks, Mr. Gomez," I said. I felt a little better. "See you later."

As I crossed the street, I saw **Nick** in his front yard. His mom was home. I didn't have to watch him, but I invited him to the meeting anyway.

"Do you want to come over to my house and help Peter?" I asked.

"Yeah," Nick said. "Peter treats me like **a big kid.**"

Everyone came to the tree house. Even Adam.

"I told my coach I had to help Peter," Adam explained. "**Friends are more important than football.**"

"Thanks, Adam," Peter said. "But you should go to practice so you don't get kicked off the team. My campaign is **HOPELESS.**"

"How come?" Nick asked. He looked worried.

"I haven't done a very good job of telling people why they should vote for me," Peter explained.

"I'll tell them," **Nick** said. "Just give me the phone numbers."

"You're a GENIUS, Nick!" I exclaimed.
"Calling people is a great idea."

"A last-minute phone call will tell everyone about Peter's ideas," Monica said.

"Exactly," I said. "This campaign isn't over until the voting starts."

"What will we say?" Tommy asked.

"We can just explain Peter's ideas and tell people why they should vote for him," Becca said. "I think that once people *really hear* his ideas, they'll want to vote for him."

"Exactly!" I said. **"This election isn't over yet!"**

My mom had a copy of the school directory, so we just divided it up. I took L – P. Then we all went home to call people for Peter.

CHAPTER 14

The Big Push

The **big push** to get Peter elected was on! The next day at school, we all gathered by Peter's locker. The election was the next day, Friday. Thursday was our last day to campaign for Peter.

Peter had a paper sign pinned on his T-shirt. It read:

A Vote for Peter is a Vote for T-shirt Tuesday!

Monica and I had extra "Vote For Peter" signs. Just in case someone wanted to carry one around school. Becca had stickers. Tommy had more fliers.

The other candidates were trying to get more votes, too. The football team (minus Adam) marched up and down the hall. They chanted, "Vote for Brad! Vote for Brad!" Anna's committee gave away **doughnut holes**. I didn't see any signs for Jenny.

Kyle and his friends were carrying signs that said:

Short Kids For Peter!

"We all hope you win," Kyle told Peter.

"**A stool at every water fountain!**" Peter said.
Then he wandered away, trying to talk to people.

Other kids had signs for Peter too.

Academic Club Supports Peter!

No surrender! No retreat!
The History Club will vote for Pete!

The Math Club says:
"Make your vote count – Vote for Peter Wiggins!"

I did a double take when I saw Sylvia. She was walking (ever so slowly) with a sign that said:

Anna's ex-workers for Peter!

"Did you quit Anna's committee, **Sylvia?**" I asked.

"Anna is too **BOSSY**," Sylvia said.

"Uh oh," Monica said. "Here comes **trouble**."

I looked where Monica pointed.

Jenny was walking toward me. She had a sign resting on her shoulder.

"She looks MAD," I whispered. I was terrified, but I stayed where I was.

Jenny stopped right in front of me.

"I have one thing to say to you, Claudia," she growled.

"What?" I squeaked.

Then an amazing thing happened.

Jenny Pinski smiled.

"I hope Peter beats Anna by a mile," Jenny said. She showed us her sign. It said:

Vote for Peter.

Jenny Pinski is.

"Did you drop out of the race?" I asked.

"I only ran because I don't want Anna to win," Jenny admitted. "Peter will make a **great president**."

Jenny walked away. Her campaign committee followed her. They were all carrying Peter signs.

I looked at Monica. "Do you think Peter can win?" I asked quietly.

"Maybe," Monica said. "A lot of kids are glad an ordinary guy is running."

Peter ran back to us. He talked really fast.

"Jenny Pinski wants me to win!" he yelled. "And kids I don't know are wishing me luck. Did you see all the Peter signs?"

"It's really cool," I said.

"Thank you so much, Claudia," **Peter** said. "I can't believe so many kids are cheering for me. I'm not a loser, even if I lose the election."

I still really wanted him to win.

* * *

On Friday morning, Peter's friends met outside homeroom.

"This is it," I said. "Election day."

Tommy slapped Peter on the back and said, "You're plain old *Peter now*, but on Monday you might be **President Peter**."

Peter smiled. "No matter what happens, I'll never forget how hard you all worked," he told us. "**It's been a blast**."

"So you're not sorry you ran?" I asked.

"No!" Peter said, laughing. "I have a bunch of new friends."

"Just don't forget your old ones," Adam joked.

"No way," Peter said.

I felt FANTASTIC in homeroom, when Ms. Stark said it was time to vote. I felt even better when **I voted for Peter.**

CHAPTER 15

P.S.

The election went just like everyone expected:

The athletes all voted for Brad. The in-crowd voted for Anna. Everyone else voted for Peter. But everyone else is a lot of votes!

There are more regular kids than cheerleaders. And there are more regular kids than athletes. Since all of the regular kids voted for Peter, he **WON!**

How did the other candidates feel about losing?

Brad was relieved. He really was too busy to be president. Anna was embarrassed, because she lost big to Peter! Jenny was thrilled that Peter won. And she was thrilled that Anna was embarrassed.

Oh, and Adam was not kicked off the football team for skipping practice to come to our emergency committee meeting. His coach was proud he had worked on Peter's campaign.

His coach said, **"Democracy doesn't work unless people work for democracy."**

About the Author

Diana G. Gallagher lives in Florida with her husband and five dogs, four cats, and a cranky parrot. Her hobbies are gardening, garage sales, and grandchildren. She has been an English equitation instructor, a professional folk musician, and an artist. However, she had aspirations to be a professional writer at the age of twelve. She has written dozens of books for kids and young adults.

About the Illustrator

Brann Garvey lives in Minneapolis, Minnesota with his wife, Keegan, and their very fat cat, Iggy. Brann graduated from Iowa State University with a bachelor of fine arts degree. He later attended the Minneapolis College of Art and Design, where he studied illustration. In his free time, Brann enjoys being with his family and friends. He brings his sketchbook everywhere he goes.

Glossary

bribery (BRIBE-ur-ee)—offering someone money or gifts so that they will do something for you

campaign (kam-PAYN)—a plan to win an election

candidate (KAN-duh-date)—someone who is running in an election

catastrophe (kuh-TASS-truh-fee)—a terrible disaster

committee (kuh-MIT-ee)—people working together

debate (di-BATE)—a discussion between people with different views

democracy (di-MOK-ruh-see)—a system of government in which the people elect the leaders

election (i-LEK-shuhn)—choosing someone or deciding something by voting

headquarters (HED-quor-turz)—the place from which an organization is run

nominate (NOM-uh-nate)—suggest that someone would be the right person to do a job

pander (PAN-dur)—do something just to make someone happy or so that they will do what you want

slogans (SLOH-guhnz)—phrases or mottos used to show goals and beliefs

Discussion Questions

1. Why does Claudia think Peter would be a good president?

2. Why do you think Peter didn't want his friends to second his nomination?

3. Whose fault was it when Anna stole Peter's campaign slogans for her posters? Why?

Writing Prompts

1. If you were running for class president, what promises would you make? Explain your answers.

2. If you went to Claudia's school, which candidate would you vote for: Jenny, Peter, Brad, or Anna? Why?

3. Are there class presidents in your school? How are they chosen? Do you like the way they are chosen or not?

MORE FUN
with Claudia!

FRIENDS FOREVER?

THE COMPLICATED LIFE OF
Claudia
Cristina
Cortez
BY DIANA G. GALLAGHER

STONE ARCH *Realistic Fiction*

THE COMPLICATED LIFE OF
Claudia
Cristina
Cortez
BY DIANA G. GALLAGHER

PARTY!

STONE ARCH *Realistic Fiction*

Claudia Cristina Cortez

Just like every other thirteen-year-old girl, Claudia Cristina Cortez has a complicated life. Whether she's studying for the big Quiz Show, babysitting her neighbor, Nick, avoiding mean Jenny Pinski, planning the seventh-grade dance, or trying desperately to pass the swimming test at camp, Claudia goes through her complicated life with confidence, cleverness, and a serious dash of cool.

WHATEVER JOURNAL

David Mortimore Baxter

David is a great kid, but he has one big problem — he can't stop talking. These wildly humorous stories, told by David himself, will show you just how much trouble a boy and his mouth can get into, whether he's making promises to become class president or bragging that he's best friends with the world's most famous wrestler. David is fun, engaging, cool, and smart enough to realize that growing up is the biggest adventure of all.

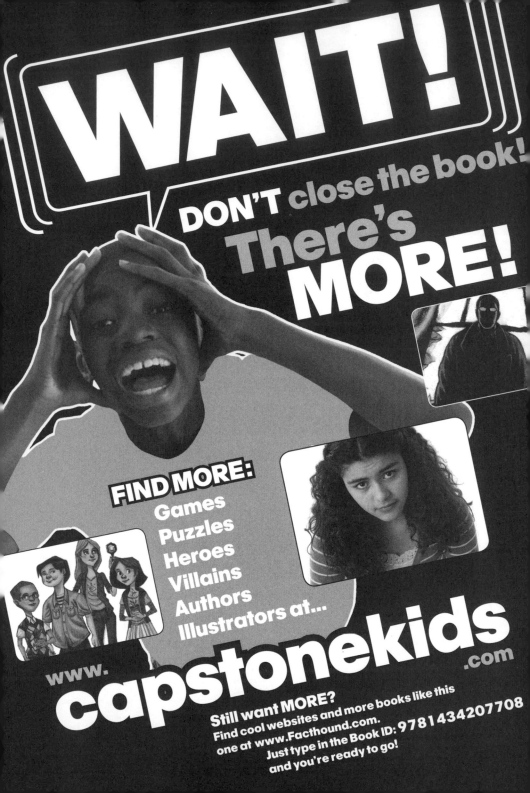